The Snowman

Raymond Briggs

HAMISH HAMILTON

PUFFIN

HAMISH HAMILTON/PUFFIN

Published by the Penguin Group
Penguin Books Ltd, 27 Wrights Lane, London W8 5TZ, England
Penguin Putnam Inc., 375 Hudson Street, New York, New York 10014, USA
Penguin Books Australia Ltd, Ringwood, Victoria, Australia
Penguin Books Canada Ltd, 10 Alcorn Avenue, Toronto, Ontario, Canada M4V 3B2
Penguin Books (NZ) Ltd, Private Bag 102902, NSMC, Auckland, New Zealand

Penguin Books Ltd, Registered Offices: Harmondsworth, Middlesex, England

First published by Hamish Hamilton Ltd 1978
Published in Puffin Books 1980

This edition published by Hamish Hamilton Ltd 1998
9 10 8

Published in Puffin Books 1998
1 3 5 7 9 10 8 6 4 2

Copyright © Raymond Briggs, 1978

Printed in Italy by Printer Trento Srl

British Library Cataloguing in Publication Data
A CIP catalogue record for this book is available from the British Library

ISBN 0–241–13938–4 Hardback
ISBN 0–140–50350–1 Paperback

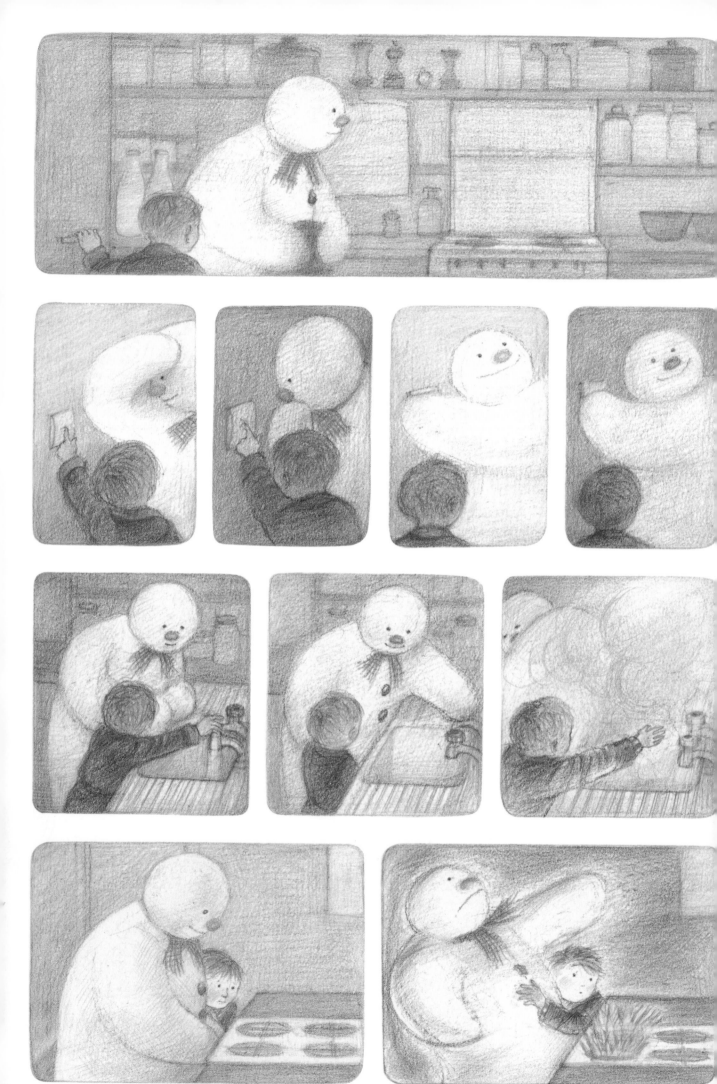

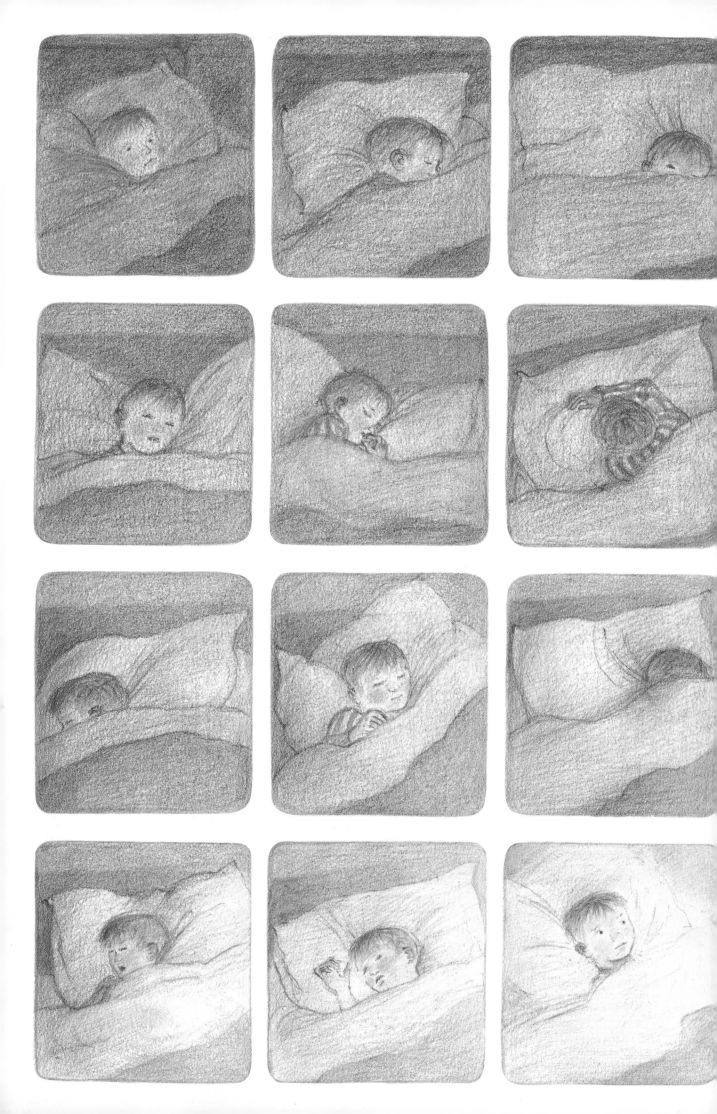